This igloo book belongs to:

....

igloobooks

Original story by Robert Louis Stevenson
Retold by Helen Catt
Illustrated by Eva Morales

Cover designed by Lee Italiano
Interiors designed by Justine Ablett
Edited by Hannah Cather

An imprint of Bonnier Publishing USA
251 Park Avenue South, New York, New York 10010

Manufactured in China. FIR003 1017
10 9 8 7 6 5 4 3 2 1

Library of Congress Cataloging-in-Publication
Data is available upon request.

ISBN 978-1-4998-8006-9
IglooBooks.com
bonnierpublishingusa.com

Treasure Island

igloobooks

I am Jim Hawkins and my tale begins when I was a young boy, at my father's inn, the Admiral Benbow. It was there that I first met an old sailor called Billy Bones.

"Fifteen men on the dead man's chest. Yo-ho-ho and a bottle of rum!" Billy sang as he showed me an old treasure map. He told tales of pirates and the hidden treasure of the long-dead Captain Flint.
"It's the map the pirates want," Billy muttered.

Soon after, Billy died suddenly. It was then that I resolved to take his map and sail with my trusted friend, Captain Smollett, to find Treasure Island for myself.

At Bristol docks, I saw the famous trading ship, the Hispaniola, for the first time. Aboard the ship, the crew was busy making ready to set sail.

I felt a thrill of excitement as I clambered along the gangplank, but as I boarded, Captain Smollett beckoned me over.

"I don't trust this crew," he whispered to me.

"Shiver me timbers!" boomed a voice behind us. It was that of Long John Silver.

Billy Bones had warned me about this one-legged sailor, but Long John was so friendly that I soon forgot my fears.

Then, one day, I went to fetch an apple from a barrel in the ship's kitchen. As I reached in, the ship rolled over a wave and shuddered. I suddenly **tumbled** headlong into the barrel.

Just then, I heard Long John come into the kitchen, slyly whispering to another sailor.

"Someone on this ship has the map to Flint's treasure," he hissed to the sailor. "We were Flint's crew and it's ours by right. When we see land, you stay aboard and take the ship. I'll find the treasure."

At that moment, the lookout in the crow's nest shouted, **"Land, ho!"** We had found Treasure Island.

The crew scrambled on deck and I rushed to the helm to find Smollett. **"Captain,"** I whispered. **"Long John Silver is planning a mutiny."**

Smollett nodded and whispered to me, **"Don't worry, Jim, I have a plan."**

"Silver!" shouted Smollett. **"Take some men and go ashore. We need water and supplies."**

Determined to discover the pirates' plans, I hid in their boat as they cast off. As we neared the beach, Silver muttered threats against Smollett and the crew. Suddenly, he spotted me. In a panic, I dived into the water and swam to shore. I heard Silver shout after me, but I was too terrified to look back.

Once ashore, I ran to the forest and wandered for some time. Suddenly, a blast of cannon fire sent birds flapping into the sky. I paused for breath and heard a strange rustling in the shadows. A figure flitted like a deer between the trees.

"Who's there?"
I shouted nervously.

A man with a shaggy beard stepped forward. "My name is
Ben Gunn," he said hoarsely. "Pirates marooned me here
years ago. That's not Flint's ship, is it?"
"Flint is dead," I said, "but his old crew are leading a mutiny."

Ben agreed to help, if I promised him passage back home.

Ben led me along a marshy trail, between willows and tall bulrushes. On a craggy hill, I saw a British flag flying. **"That'll be your friends,"** said Ben.

We climbed the hill and saw a wooden fort surrounded with pointed stakes.

"Jim!" Smollett shouted from the lookout. I rushed inside and Ben followed.

"It's good to see you," Smollett said when I introduced Ben. Smollett told us how, after Long John Silver had gone ashore, the pirates left aboard mutinied. Those still loyal to Smollett escaped on a rowboat, which the pirates sank with a cannonball. They had swum ashore, found Flint's old fort, and set up camp there.

We waited in the fort until, some time later, a figure appeared with a white flag. "I've come to talk," said Long John cautiously, stepping forward a few paces. "If you give us that treasure map, I give you my word of honor that we'll leave you alone. We'll even take you back to England when we've found the treasure. Do we have a deal?"

Long John smiled, but Smollett's face looked like thunder.
"Good men don't make deals with pirates," he said
and turned his back on Long John Silver.

Suddenly we heard the pirates shout as they ran forward, swords drawn.

"HOLD THE FORT!" the Captain ordered. We each grabbed a cutlass, ready to fight. But we had forgotten that Flint's old crew had built the fort, and Long John knew a secret entrance.

The pirates swarmed through the hidden passage and Captain Smollett gave the order to flee. I turned to run with the others, but someone grabbed me roughly by the shirt and pulled me back.

"Captain!" I shouted, but no one heard me over the commotion.

"Hello, Jim," said Long John Silver. "I believe you have something we want." I struggled, but the pirate held me firm. "You'll get nothing from me!" I cried, but as I spoke, another buccaneer took my knapsack and pulled out the map. The pirates cheered and my heart sank to my boots.

"No hard feelings, Jim," Silver whispered as we walked along the marshy path. "Now, let's make a deal. If one more thing goes wrong, these scurvy dogs will turn against me. But you're better than that. I'll stand by you and keep you safe, if, when the time comes, you stand by me."

We reached the grove where three tall pine trees stood, as shown on the map. All we found there was a hole in the ground, full of empty chests and cases. The pirates leaped into the pit, digging with their fingers, but found just a single two-guinea piece.

"Two guineas! That's all that's left of the treasure!"

one of the pirates shouted. **"That black-hearted scoundrel brought us here for nothing, and now we'll be arrested and tried for mutiny."** They turned on us, swords and cutlasses drawn.

"Run, Jim!"
shouted Silver.

Crack! Crack! Crack!

Three musket shots flashed out of the thicket and Smollett, Ben, and the rest of the crew burst into the clearing.

The pirates scrambled out of the pit and drew their swords. Long John handed me one of his pistols and we took aim, ready to fire.

One by one, the pirates dropped their swords. They put their hands up and backed away, until they disappeared among the trees.

"Quick, men," Smollett said, "find their rowboats and destroy all but one. We can't have them going back to the ship."

The crew rushed off to obey his orders.

"What happened to the treasure?" I asked.

"Follow me," said Ben, grinning.

We went to his cave, where, behind a little pool of clear water, glittered gold and silver bars, and thousands of strange coins from all corners of the world. It was Flint's treasure.

In his lonely wanderings about the island, Ben had found the treasure and carried it to his cave. When I was kidnapped, Ben had told Smollett that the treasure was gone, and so Smollett and his men had hidden in wait at the grove, ready to ambush the pirates when they arrived.

We gathered what we could and carried it to the ship. It was weary work, and when the sun started to set, we decided to leave the rest behind. We had more than we could ever spend.

The mutinous pirates were left on the shore, marooned just as Ben had been. All except Long John, that was. We had made a deal to stand by each other. He had honored that deal when we had discovered the missing treasure. Now it was my turn to stand by him, so when we set sail to England, he came with us.

Early one morning, while everyone was sleeping, I heard a soft splash. I crept above deck and, peering over the side, saw that Long John Silver was silently rowing away. He had a sack of coins at his feet, glinting in the early morning sun, and that was the last I ever saw of him.

But I still see the island in my dreams. I wake in the night, hearing the boom of cannons, the crashing of waves against the shore, or the whispering of those wild woods. There is still treasure there, in Ben Gunn's cave, but as long as I live, I'll never return to Treasure Island.

Discover three more enchanting classic tales. . . .

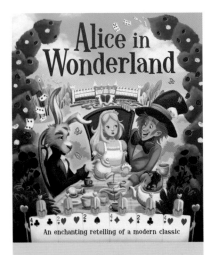

Alice in Wonderland

An enchanting retelling of a modern classic

Join Alice and tumble down the rabbit hole into Wonderland, where nothing is as it seems. This beautiful book is perfect for creating the most magical of storytimes for every little reader.

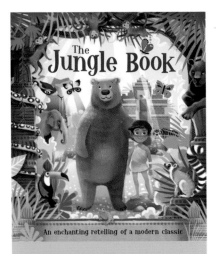

The Jungle Book

An enchanting retelling of a modern classic

Join Mowgli as he learns the strange ways of the jungle, ever guided by the wise bear, Baloo. This retelling of the timeless classic, with beautiful illustrations, will capture every child's imagination.

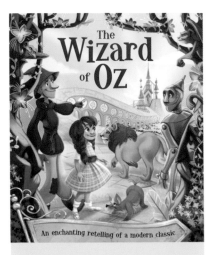

The Wizard of Oz

An enchanting retelling of a modern classic

Be swept away with Dorothy and Toto to the Land of Oz, where they meet a talking Scarecrow, Tin Man, and Lion. This retelling of the well-loved classic tale is sure to make storytime exciting.

Look out for these other exciting tales in our storytime series!

igloobooks